PUFFIN BOOKS

RAGDOLLY ANNA

Ragdolly Anna is a very special doll, even though she's only made from a morsel of this and a tatter of that. She not only learns to walk and talk, but from the moment she begins to live with the Little Dressmaker, the White Cat and Dummy, she has the most amazing adventures.

Within hours of starting life she is kidnapped by mice, but later she is rescued by a frog and locked up in a museum, and she even finds herself sledging on a tin tray.

These six stories about Ragdolly Anna and her friends, which have been filmed by Yorkshire Television, will delight readers of five to seven and are perfect for reading aloud.

Illustrated by Jane Hughes

Jean Kenward

*

RAGDOLLY ANNA

Puffin Books

Puffin Books, Penguin Books Ltd, Harmondsworth, Middlesex, England
Penguin Books, 40 West 23rd Street, New York, New York 10010, U.S.A.
Penguin Books Australia Ltd, Ringwood, Victoria, Australia
Penguin Books Canada Ltd, 2801 John Street, Markham, Ontario, Canada L3R 1B4
Penguin Books (N.Z.) Ltd, 182–190 Wairau Road, Auckland 10, New Zealand

First published by Frederick Warne 1979
Published in Puffin Books 1984

Copyright © Jean Kenward, 1979
Illustrations copyright © Jane Hughes, 1984
All rights reserved

Made and printed in Great Britain by
Richard Clay (The Chaucer Press) Ltd,
Bungay, Suffolk
Filmset in Monophoto Baskerville by
Northumberland Press Ltd, Gateshead, Tyne and Wear

Contents

*

Ragdolly Anna

*

On the fifth floor of a block of flats in the middle of a certain city there lived a Little Dressmaker. Having neither husband nor children, she made a home for herself with a cat, a geranium, and a large dining-room table with curly legs. On the table sat a sewing machine, and in a corner of the room facing the light stood a tailor's Dummy. It was as big as a woman, and the same shape, too, only there was a handle in the middle of its back. When the Little Dressmaker turned the handle one way, the Dummy grew fatter and fatter. When she turned it the other, the Dummy shrank till it was really quite thin. Then you could easily feel sorry for it. But the Dummy was happy, for the Dressmaker often talked to it, when she sat alone working at her sewing. She had made it a cap, too, to conceal the fact that it had no hair, and had marked on its face a couple of eyes, a blob of a nose, and a mouth that looked as if it might smile – when nobody was looking. The Dummy was a lady – anybody could see that.

The Little Dressmaker worked hard. She would lay a tray for breakfast with a neat cloth for she liked things to be nice. When she had finished her boiled egg and her tea she would shake the crumbs carefully off her lap, and pour a little milk into a saucer for the cat. It was a White Cat and particular.

Then she would begin to sew. She was nimble with her fingers, and many people brought material for her to make up into overcoats and school tunics, nightdresses and gentlemen's shirts; but best of all were the ball gowns. The Little Dressmaker liked doing these. She would smooth the material lovingly, and hold it up against the tailor's Dummy, having first wound her in or out according to the customer's size. Sometimes the satin, or silk, or velvet would sprawl over the table for days, under a sheath of tissue paper to keep off the dust. When she had finished a ball gown, and packed it off to its owner, the Little Dressmaker would sit by the fire of an evening with her skirt turned back over her knees, to let in the warmth. She would imagine the ballroom, the lights, the music, the gentlemen in their black coats and medals, the ladies in their exquisite gowns.

'Mine will be the best,' she would assure herself. And her eyes would shine, as she stroked the White Cat who kept her company. 'Miaouw,' he would reply. 'Miaouw!'

One morning, when the air seemed full of winter, and a pale sun shone in the windows of the flat on the fifth floor, the Little Dressmaker decided to go through her materials and tidy up. Some she put in a pile marked 'Rummage'. Some she labelled simply 'Throw away'. Some had a ticket saying 'Useful'. But when all the piles were completed, there were still a few bits left: a morsel of this, and a tatter of that – too small for rummage, too pretty to be thrown away, and too mixed up to be useful. 'I know!' decided the Little Dressmaker, 'I'll make a rag doll!'

So she did. First she cut out the body; there was a length of brown stockinette which did beautifully for that. Then she sewed the face. It was important that the doll should have a pleasant expression, and she spent quite a long time stitching blue eyes, white teeth, and a red mouth. Then she cut some squiggly lengths of twine to make hair. The rag doll began to wake up. Soon she was dressed in a vest and bloomers, a petticoat with lace on, and a cotton gown. The Little Dressmaker knitted a shawl to keep her shoulders warm; and to finish her off she made a tiny straw hat out of an old raffia table mat. In the hat she stuck a bunch of paper roses.

'She must have a name,' mused the Little Dressmaker, putting the lid on the sewing machine, and preparing herself a drink of hot milk. 'What shall it be? Daisy? Veronica? Mabel? No – they just don't sound right. She is too brown for a daisy, and too gay for Veronica. I know – Ragdolly Anna! That's it! That's what we'll call her!'

She clapped her hands. Ragdolly Anna was put to bed in a boot box.

That night there was a full moon. It shone through the windows of the flat on the fifth floor, and lit up the room as brightly as if it were day. The White Cat went to visit a friend on a neighbouring balcony. My, it was cold! The Dummy was standing quite still in the corner ... but what was that, fidgeting behind the rag bag? What was that, nibbling a hole in the boot box where Ragdolly Anna slept? A family of mice lived under the floorboards. They knew that the White Cat was out visiting so they had come to investigate.

'Ma – there's something in here. It ain't cheese!'

'Ma – it's a *person*. It's got roses in its hat!'

They gnawed round the edge of the hole until there was quite a large opening.

'Get out of the way, children! Let your parents go in first. Such manners! And you never know – it might be dangerous!'

Ragdolly Anna did not look dangerous. She smiled. It was dull in the boot box. She was quite glad of company.

'It's an angel, that's what it is,' fussed the mother mouse. 'It's an angel that's fallen out of the sky. Just fancy that!'

'It'd look nice, Ma, standing in our hallway,' squeaked the father mouse. 'Not everyone has an angel in the hall. Let's get it out of the box. Now then, all together, *gnaw*!'

The young mice gnawed obediently. They were so excited that their teeth made short work of the boot box. Over by the window, the tailor's Dummy stared at them, but she could not run to the assistance of Ragdolly Anna because she had no legs.

Ragdolly Anna had two very good legs, but she hadn't learnt to use them yet. She wished she had been able to run away because the mice were beginning to be unpleasant.

'Now we've got her.' The father mouse took Ragdolly Anna's shawl in his teeth and pulled. The mother mouse pushed. The baby mice jumped up and down and got in the way and fell over each other. One of them actually ran up the tailor's Dummy, and I am sure that in her empty old nut of a head she thought, 'Such rudeness!'

The mice began to drag Ragdolly Anna across

the floor. When they got to the mouse hole they ran into difficulties. Ragdolly Anna was too big to go through the hole! The mice tried gnawing at it a bit, but they didn't want to make it too wide for fear of the cat. They pushed and squeezed poor Ragdolly Anna until most of her body was through, but no matter how they pushed and pulled and struggled, the straw hat with the paper roses would not go in. In the end they actually had to snap a bit off the brim to make it smaller.

At last – plop! Ragdolly Anna disappeared down the mouse hole. Only just in time. It was morning.

The Little Dressmaker shivered as she got out of bed. There had been a hard frost. She dressed quickly, for she was pleased about the rag doll. 'It will make a splendid Christmas present,' she decided. 'I must wrap it up in coloured paper and give it to myself. Oh! What has happened? Who has been nibbling the boot box? Ragdolly Anna has GONE!'

Well – there was a fine to-do, and no mistake. Such a mess! Scraps of cardboard box lay scattered all over the carpet. What was to be done? First, the Little Dressmaker fetched her dustpan, and tidied everything up. Then she telephoned the police.

The police came, four of them, in a van with a hooter. They marched up to the fifth floor in their heavy lace-up boots, and they searched *everywhere* for Ragdolly Anna. They even took the head off the tailor's Dummy and looked inside her; but there was nothing there except some iron things like ribs, and a piece of pink cotton, and a scrap of apple core. The tailor's Dummy felt all airy and peculiar without her head, and she was glad when they put it on again. But she could not speak. She could not tell them that Ragdolly Anna had been carried away by marauders. They looked and looked – in the coal scuttle, in the teapot, in the Wellington boots, behind the gas-stove ... NOTHING!

Then they straightened their uniforms and picked up their helmets, and went home.

Under the floorboards it was dark – as dark as midnight, even in the afternoon. Thin cracks of light showed in the spaces where the boards did not fit very well, and where the lino had worn out, but that was all. The mouse home was not very comfortable. It was dotted with little heaps of this and that, broken buttons, lengths of bacon rind, scraps of newspaper they had found in the wastepaper basket, and there was everywhere a strong smell of mouse. Ugh! Some people did not believe in washing, and they had no bathroom. Ragdolly Anna didn't like it at all. She was propped up in the hall, wedged, so that she could not fall down, and some cobwebs were twined round her, tastefully, from corner to corner.

'Now she looks like a queen,' said the father mouse, with satisfaction. He rubbed his paws together, and gave a little jump.

Weeks passed. The Little Dressmaker was busy. The mystery of the rag doll had never been solved; she hadn't the heart to make another. All day long she worked at her sewing. The wheel went round and around – *WWRRRRRRRRrrrrrr*. The tailor's Dummy was made fatter or thinner, *crink, crank*. Soon it was Christmas. A new feeling came into the flat on the fifth floor. A feeling of pine needles, and sticky paper, and mince pies. A feeling of excitement. The room was decorated with paper chains. The tailor's Dummy wore a bit of tinsel in her cap, and a muslin skirt to disguise the fact that she had no legs.

'Hark, the herald angels sing!' called the carol singers.

Sweeping the floor, late one evening, the Little Dressmaker found a bit of raffia that looked uncommonly like Ragdolly Anna's hat. 'You see?' she cried out. The White Cat miaouwed. Yes, he saw. Then he sniffed. His three-cornered nose twitched. His fur stood up straight. His tail waved from side to side. 'Mice!' he growled. 'Miaouw! Mice! The audacity of them! Living here – right under my nose! Mind you, I have had rather a bad cold lately!'

He began to prowl round the flat, sniffing . . . sniffing, and twitching. The Little Dressmaker followed, holding her skirt close about her knees, for you never knew . . . When they reached the mouse hole, they stopped and listened.

Someone was playing a piano. It must have been a very tiny piano, for the notes sounded as high and thin as icicles. Someone was playing a flute. It must have been a very tiny flute, for it sounded no louder than the wind does when you blow through a lemonade straw. (I think, myself, that it *was* a lemonade straw, for the father mouse was quick and nifty, and often stole things.) *Tra-la ... tra-la ... tra-la ... la,* sounded from underneath the floorboards. There was a giggle of mouse laughter.

'Don't! You shouldn't! Oh, you *are* naughty! Oh!' Then there was the sound of a kiss, a bang, and more giggles.

The mice were celebrating Christmas. Soon they began to sing. The Little Dressmaker put her ear to the mouse hole, and held her breath. This is what she heard:

> We've got a dolly
> that's made of stuff,
> filled with feathers
> and bits of fluff;
> eyes she has,
> and stocking feet,
> and a shawl to keep
> her shoulders neat.
>
> This rag dolly
> is fine and brown;
> she can't stand up
> and she won't sit down.
> This rag dolly
> is fine and fat,
> with a bunch of paper roses
> in her big straw hat!

Suddenly the song stopped.

'There's a cat about!' whispered father mouse hoarsely. 'Get away, all of you. Quickly, now. Through the escape routes, into the larder. Skedaddle! Run!'

A great deal of scuffling and squeaking followed.

'Take your plimsolls, lovey!' called the mother mouse. 'Don't forget the eiderdown – the one that I stuffed with the Little Dressmaker's hair combings! Run, now! Run!'

There was a final scutter of bodies tumbling over each other in an effort to get away, and then silence.

The Little Dressmaker peered down the mouse hole. 'I can't see any mice,' she whispered, 'but I can see Ragdolly Anna. How shall we rescue her?'

The White Cat sniffed. 'We're both too big and too clean to go scuffling about in mouse holes. I know! I have it! Nutcrackers!'

'What?' queried the Little Dressmaker.

'We'll poke the nutcrackers down the hole, and pick up Ragdolly Anna with their two pincers. It'll be easy. Brains – that's what you need,' advised the White Cat haughtily. 'I should have been a detective.'

Together, they found the nutcrackers which had been polished ready for Christmas. Holding the handles gingerly, the Little Dressmaker pushed them into the hole . . . down . . . down . . . down . . . until she felt something soft.

'Ow!' cried Ragdolly Anna. 'It's me! Mind! Mind my hat!'

'Gently does it,' mewed the White Cat. 'This way – let me help. A little to the left – a little to the right – squeeze – pull . . . That's it. Up she comes!'

Out came Ragdolly Anna. What a sight! She was covered with cobwebs. The lace on her petticoat was torn, her ribbons were tangled, her shawl was in tatters, and her hat was on one side. Some of the paper roses had been taken off. (I suspect the mice had used them for bedcovers.) But she was smiling. It was good to be in the light again, after so many weeks of dust and darkness.

What a welcome she had, to be sure! The Little Dressmaker set to work immediately, and made her some new clothes: a velvet cloak, a gown of rose-coloured satin, fresh paper roses for her hat. She even cut out a tiny, tiny lace handkerchief and put it in her pocket.

And she gave her a cup of hot chicken soup.

When night came, and they were all going to bed, the Little Dressmaker did not pack Ragdolly Anna into a boot box. Instead, she made a place for her on the pillow beside her. 'She will be under my eye,' she explained to the White Cat.

'Quite right,' he agreed, wrinkling his nose. 'Mice, indeed! I shall have to do sentry duty in future.'

Over by the window, the tailor's Dummy let out a faint creak. She would have said 'Hooray!' if she could, but we cannot all be so clever.

Only some of us.

CREAK!

Ragdolly Anna
and the Bacon

*

From Christmas until Easter is a long time. The Little Dressmaker finished off her ball gowns, and started on summer dresses. Dummy wore checked gingham one day, striped seersucker the next; she went out and in at such a rate that she was really hard put to it remembering what size she had been to begin with. It was quite surprising that she did not develop a bad temper. But she never frowned, or shouted, or even cried '*Ow*!' when a pin was stuck in rather further than usual. Her mouth always seemed as if it might smile when nobody was looking.

Sometimes the Little Dressmaker would get overtired. Then things would go wrong: she might prick her finger, or sew on a button instead of a popper, or put in a zip upside down. She would mutter, 'Bother!' or 'Fiddle, faddle!' and stamp her foot. The White Cat arched its back at such moments, and waved its tail grandly from side to side, or took offence and went to visit its relations. Ragdolly Anna peeped over the edge of the eiderdown.

But Dummy stayed still, with her 'almost smile' on her face. I don't think she ever had a cross thought in her head.

Ragdolly Anna, though, was becoming quite clever. She had learnt to walk, and every day the Little Dressmaker gave her conversation lessons. They began with such phrases as 'Good morning!' and 'How do you do?' She grew very good at these. She used to lie awake at night and practise them quietly, under her breath, while the Little Dressmaker was sleeping.

'Good morning!' she would whisper – to the moon, maybe, or to the curtains – and then, rather politely, 'How do you do?' Soon she had learned quite a lot of words, and the Little Dressmaker made her a tiny notebook to write them down in. First all the words that began with an a, such as apple, and alphabet, and abracadabra. Then boats and bricks and biscuits. And so on, through cats and cricket bats to doughnuts and dice; from doughnuts to elephants and from elephants all the way to zebras, with I don't know how many words in the middle. Ragdolly Anna liked her conversation lessons, and sometimes, for a treat, the Little Dressmaker would teach her a really long word, like EXTRA-

ORDINARY. And once she told Ragdolly Anna her own special favourite – UMPTIMACDOUDELOUS. Ragdolly Anna thought it was a splendid word. She asked the Little Dressmaker what it meant.

'It means "rum",' she explained.

Ragdolly Anna said that she thought rum was something to drink.

'No, not *that* sort of rum,' the Little Dressmaker went on. '*Rum*, meaning odd or strange.'

'Or EXTRAORDINARY,' said Ragdolly Anna.

'Exactly,' said the Little Dressmaker.

When she had learned her words, and the Little Dressmaker had settled to her sewing, Ragdolly Anna would walk up and down admiring herself in the looking glass. Of course, she always wore the same clothes: the rose-coloured gown, the velvet cloak, the petticoat and bloomers. But it was the hat that gave her the greatest pleasure. Ragdolly Anna had a special round cardboard box to keep it in at night. It had once been a pill box. But she was so fond of her hat that she wore it every day, even in the bath, and at mealtimes. She put it on when she got up.

'You never know when you may be called to go out in a hurry,' she would say. She never *did* go out, for the Little Dressmaker was afraid that she might get lost. Or maybe somebody would steal her, or push her over.

Most of the day, Ragdolly Anna sat on the balcony, watching the people go by far, far below. Living in a flat five flights up meant that you felt a bit like a bird. You saw the tops of things, instead of their underneaths. That could be interesting, especially when a fire engine rattled past, or an important visitor came to see the Queen. There was a lift in the flats, but it very seldom worked, so when the Little Dressmaker went out to do her shopping, she had to go down five flights of stairs before she was out in the street. Each time, Ragdolly Anna and the White Cat said goodbye, and then hurried to the window to wave. They had to wait quite a long time

before she appeared in the bottom doorway with her shopping basket. She always turned round and looked up to wave back at them before she trotted round to the supermarket.

'I wish I could go with her,' sighed Ragdolly Anna.

'That is stupid,' said the White Cat, washing behind its left ear very carefully. 'We are as we are. Some of us are designed to go shopping. Some are not. For my part, I consider myself far too superior for such antics. Let *her* buy our dinner and bring it home and serve it up in a saucer. That is best.'

Dummy said nothing, but stared into a corner of the room, with that 'almost smile' on her face.

One morning, after the Little Dressmaker had been out for quite a long time, and had trundled up the five flights of stairs with a basketful of groceries, she found she had dropped a packet of bacon in the High Street.

'Oh dear! It's most unfortunate,' she sighed. 'I know I had it when I came out of the shop. I can't spare the time to go all the way back and fetch it. Whatever shall we do? There'll be nothing for dinner – that's certain.'

Ragdolly Anna gave a little jump. 'I'll fetch it for you!' she burst out, excitedly. 'Let *me* go!'

At first the Little Dressmaker was unwilling. 'You've never been out on your own,' she explained. 'It might be dangerous. What about traffic? What about crossing the road?'

'I'll look both ways,' pleaded Ragdolly Anna. 'I promise I will. Twice.'

'What about the stairs? You can't walk down five flights by yourself.'

'I can slide down the banisters. It's easy.'

'What about the way? You don't know the way to the High Street.'

'I can read what it says on the street name-plates,' said Ragdolly Anna. 'I can read "To the Station" and "Horses Only" and "No bicycles here". High Street begins with an H.'

'I don't feel happy about it at all,' worried the Little Dressmaker. 'But *somebody* must go. The White Cat won't, *that's* for sure. Dummy is no use – she can't move at all unless I wind her handle.'

'There's only me,' persuaded Ragdolly Anna. She felt important. 'In my hat,' she added.

'All right. Be quick, mind, and don't dawdle. Hold on tight when you slide down the banisters. The bacon is streaky, love, and it's wrapped in a piece of white paper. You can't miss it.'

She watched anxiously as Ragdolly Anna tidied herself in front of the glass, and arranged her hair with care. Then she put on her straw hat with the paper roses, pulling the crown down firmly on her head so that it would not blow off.

She climbed to the top of the banisters.

26

'Hold tight!'

'I *am* holding ... tight ...'

Whoosh ... Whoosh ... Whoosh ... down and round, and down and round, and down and round, and down and round, and down again went Ragdolly Anna, until she was brought up sharp at the base of the last stairway. 'It's a good thing I pulled my hat well down,' she said to herself, slithering off the banister post and walking out of the front door.

She had never been in the street before. To begin with, it was extremely frightening. There were cars, hundreds of them, zooming this way and that. There were people, thousands of them, hurrying hither and thither. There were buildings so high that you could not see the tops of them, and streets so long that you could not see the ends of them. There were traffic lights that ordered you to STOP, GO, GET READY, GO, STOP, until you felt more like a tiddly-wink than a human being. 'And I am *nearly* human,' thought Ragdolly Anna, trying to get over the road safely before the lights turned green again.

She looked both ways.

The shop windows were fascinating. Never had she seen such sights! Some of them were glittering with gold rings and diamonds; they had a sort of iron netting over the glass so that thieves would not be able to break in. Others showed models of ladies about to do this or that, and wearing the most beautiful dresses while they were making up their minds. There were shops full of china, and shops full of cheeses, shops full of bananas and shops full of books. Ragdolly Anna hurried up Church Street and down Hill Street, round the roundabout where seven red buses were stuck in a circle, and at last – yes – there was a notice saying 'HIGH STREET' quite loud and clear, as if everybody were look-ing at it, or if they weren't, they ought to be.

If you are only just tall enough to fit in a boot box, people aren't very likely to notice you on a crowded pavement. Ragdolly Anna ran in and out of a great number of legs – legs with trousers on them, and legs with nylon tights on them, and legs with long socks, and legs with short socks, and legs that were merely legs. Sometimes she was pushed and bumped, but not much, for she was quite nimble, and after her capture in the mouse hole she was accustomed to difficulties of size and shape.

The bacon was lying by the kerb, still wrapped up neatly in white paper, and with a label on it which said 'Streaky'.

'That's good!' Ragdolly Anna had to pick it up with both hands. It was heavy – for her. She was puffing and blowing a little by then, and a bit bothered, so that when she had turned round she couldn't exactly remember which direction she had been facing when she started. Nevertheless, she set off, trotting briskly, and had covered at least half the way home when a large drop of rain fell on her hat and made it wobble.

Ragdolly Anna looked at the sky. It had become dark all over. The blue had disappeared; a big bank of blackness was almost overhead. Another drop of rain fell, and then another, and then a whole crowd of them came tumbling down at once. They were big hard drops, like conkers. Some of the people put their umbrellas up, and you could hear THUD, THUD, *ddrrr ddrrr ddrrr* on the umbrella stuff. Ragdolly Anna had to avoid the puddles. Her pink satin gown became sadly bedraggled, her cloak clung round her, and nobody should wear a straw hat with paper roses on it when it is raining. Faster and faster she ran, and had just reached the corner of the road where the Little Dressmaker lived, five flights up, when disaster came. Trying not to get run over by a pushchair, she forgot to look where she was going, caught her foot in a large gap in the grating of a drain, and tripped. The bacon flew out of her hands, and Ragdolly Anna fell right through the hole and into the drain ... down ... down ... into utter darkness. *Flump*!

'Well! *Now* what?' Ragdolly Anna asked herself. Fortunately, there was a pile of old leaves at

the bottom of the drain, so she was not much hurt. Just bruised a little, and bewildered. Her first thought was for her hat. She took it off, tried to smooth out the soggy paper roses, and put it back on again, pulling the crown down on her head more firmly than before. One always feels braver when one is looking one's best.

She was very worried about the bacon. How was she to get out? She tried climbing up the walls of the drain, but they were slippery, and she kept sliding down again. She tried building up the leaves so that they would be tall enough for her to reach the end of the grating if she were to stand on top. But there weren't enough of them. She tried calling out, 'Help! Help!' but who could hear such a tiny voice as hers? And the sound of the rain was deafening. Worse still, a trickle of water was dribbling down the drain hole, getting bigger every minute. Soon it would wash her away. And she couldn't swim. Would she ever be found.

'Help!' Her cry ended in a sob.

'What's up?' A croak sounded from somewhere in the corner.

Ragdolly Anna stared fearfully into the shadow. But she need not have been nervous. It was only an old Frog who had woken suddenly from a noonday nap. When he had got over his curiosity, he was fully prepared to be helpful. It was *his* home, after all – and the sooner this rag doll got out of it, the better.

'It's what you might call a Desirable Residence, my dear,' he explained. 'Good water supply, excellent bedding, and hardly any intruders from one day to the next. And the slugs are *admirable*. You must let me persuade you to taste one before you leave.'

Ragdolly Anna shuddered. 'I must get back to the Little Dressmaker as quickly as I can,' she said. 'Mr Frog! If only you could help me to escape!'

'One can think of a way out of anything, if one thinks *long* enough, and *hard* enough,' the Frog advised. 'I myself spend a great deal of time thinking. The darkness is helpful. No interruptions, you understand. I think and I think and I think ...'

'I do believe he's going to sleep,' thought Ragdolly Anna.

'I have it!' the Frog opened his eyes with an expression of great triumph. 'You must sit on my back, my dear, and put your arms round my neck. I have very strong hind legs. It is always so, in the Frog family. We are renowned for our jumps and leaps and gambols ... Why, I have a great uncle who leaped so high that he never came down again! Have you ever heard of such a thing?'

'No,' said Ragdolly Anna.

'When you have made yourself comfortable, and are holding on really tight, I shall jump *through* that large gap in the grating. I often do it. It's easy,' he added proudly.

Ragdolly Anna did not much like the idea of putting her arms round the Frog's neck. But after all, he was a kind old fellow. She straightened her hat, clambered up on to the Frog's great, greeny-yellowy, slimy, slithery old back, and fastened her arms round his neck. She had a peculiar feeling, as though she were frightened and excited at the same moment.

'It's a pity I haven't a parachute,' she thought, 'in case things go wrong.'

'Ready?' Gathering himself together with a series of little hops, the Frog kicked out his hind legs exactly as if they had been made of elastic, and, with one enormous leap, shot up through the gap in the grating, out into the gutter and the bright light of day!

And there on the pavement was the packet of bacon. The outside wrapping was very wet, but luckily it was also wrapped in grease-proof paper so it hadn't come to much harm.

It had stopped raining, and the sun was shining as brightly as if the whole sky had been washed clean. Ragdolly Anna had never seen it look so beautiful. Even the pavements glistened

33

and shone; and as for the gutters – a strong, whirling current pounded down them, bubbling as it went, and carrying all sorts of things with it which weren't quite sure where they were going – matchboxes and toffee papers and cigarette ends and lollipop sticks and broken pencils without any lead ...

'Lovely, isn't it?' croaked the Frog. 'Consider the worms, my dear! Consider the snails!' He hopped back to his drain, and with a clever twist, slipped down inside. But a moment later his head popped out again.

'I say!' he called.

'Yes?'

'Remember what I told you, won't you, young lady? You can find your way out of *anything* if you think long enough. Long enough, and hard enough. If you think and think and think – well, something's bound to happen. Goodbye. Drop in when you're passing.'

'Not if I know it!' thought Ragdolly Anna. But she called out, 'I'll remember, Mr Frog. And thank you very much!'

A few minutes later she had reached home.

The White Cat and the Little Dressmaker were looking out of the window. They had been feeling anxious. Ragdolly Anna had been away for a dreadfully long time. Could she have been lost? They waved, when they saw her coming. The Little Dressmaker ran to put the kettle on, and the White Cat walked carefully down the five flights of stairs to meet her.

'It's a long way to come up,' he had explained to the Little Dressmaker. 'She can hold on to my tail. And, after all, I'm very fond of bacon.'

What a rejoicing there was that dinner-time! They had chocolate blancmange for pudding to celebrate Ragdolly Anna's safe return. It was made in the shape of a rabbit. They did offer the ears to Dummy, in case she felt left out of things, but she wasn't very interested in eating and was afraid her delicately drawn mouth would get spoiled if she tried it.

When the Little Dressmaker and Ragdolly Anna were full up and comfortable, and had cleared everything away, they untied their pinafores and talked things over.

'It was a very fortunate rescue, Ragdolly Anna,' pronounced the Little Dressmaker solemnly. 'In future, we must go together when we venture on expeditions. It will be safer with two.'

Ragdolly Anna smoothed out the paper roses, and laid her hat carefully in the pill box. Her cloak was drying in front of the fire. She folded it, and started to brush out her hair. She said, 'It was EXTRAORDINARY and UMPTIMACDOUDELOUS, wasn't it?'

'Umpti *what?*' asked the White Cat, rudely.

Over by the window, Dummy stared into the corner with that 'almost smile' on her face.

She never said anything
                              at all.

Ragdolly Anna
and the River Picnic

*

'When I was a child, every summer we would have a river picnic,' said the Little Dressmaker, wetting a length of thread on her tongue, and trying to push it through the eye of the needle. It was a fine needle, with a very small eye, and she had to try a number of times before she succeeded. Pleased, she twisted a knot at the end, and looked at Ragdolly Anna over the top of her glasses. 'You've never been to the river, have you?'

Ragdolly Anna shook her head. She was tidying the button box, putting the dress buttons in one pile and the overcoat buttons in another, and the tiny pearl buttons somewhere else. They shone, and turned different colours when the light fell on them. She liked the pearl buttons best.

'On Midsummer's Day we will *go*.' The Little Dressmaker snapped her mouth shut, almost as if it were a pencil box, and her eyes twinkled. 'We'll take sandwiches. We'll get up early, and catch a bus into the country. I know a place where there are punts.'

'Punts?'

'Punts are boats with cushions in them to sit on, and long poles to push them along, stupid,' explained the White Cat, who was listening, even though he pretended to be looking the other way. 'That is what we call NAVIGATION.'

Ragdolly Anna was excited. She had seen photographs of a river, and once she had caught a glimpse of one in a picture book. But a river picnic would be something quite, quite new. How long would it be till Midsummer's Day? A week! A whole week to wait.

Ragdolly Anna cut out a calendar with seven days on it, one for each square, and hung it by her bed. Would it be fine? Would it be showery? Would it rain so hard that they might not be able to go at all?

'Stop worrying,' instructed the White Cat. 'It may rain. It may not. Who knows? I'm not a meteorological expert.' He stalked off to visit his friend on the next balcony.

Dummy said nothing, but she seemed hopeful. She usually did. She had her 'almost smile' on her face, and looked so friendly that people in the street often stopped and waved their hands to

38

her. She couldn't wave back, of course, because being a dressmaker's dummy she couldn't move her arms, but you could see that she was pleased.

On Midsummer's Eve the sun went down red and cheerful.

'Red at night, shepherds' delight,' chanted the Little Dressmaker wisely. 'We must go to bed early,' she added, 'because we have to be up with the lark. The bus leaves at eight. That will give us a nice, long day.'

Before they undressed, they got everything ready. There were quite a lot of things to prepare: sandwiches, a flask with a hot drink in it in case they felt cold, and a bottle with a cold drink

in it in case they felt hot. A packet of biscuits with icing on them, for a treat. Not chocolate, they decided, because that might melt in the sun. And two jam jars, with string on.

'What are those for?' asked Ragdolly Anna.

'Fishing,' explained the Little Dressmaker, mysteriously. 'Wait till we get there, and I'll show you.'

Then they washed themselves, and the Little Dressmaker plaited Ragdolly Anna's hair so that it would look all crinkly on the bus ride, and they went to bed. Ragdolly Anna thought she was *far* too excited to go to sleep, so she imagined some sheep getting over a stile, and counted them. By the time she had got to seventeen, she was off . . .

The alarm clock, shrilling fiercely that it was seven o'clock, woke her up.

A brilliant yellow glow shone through a crack in the curtains. She jumped out of bed, and ran to the window, and peeped out. It was a magnificent day. Anyone could see that it was midsummer. There could be no mistake about *that*.

They had boiled eggs for breakfast. Boiled eggs take three and a half minutes to cook, if you like the yellow bit to be runny. It seemed *ages* before the water bubbled . . . and I think they took the eggs out too early, because they were terribly soft and squashy. But they ate them, just the same, washed up, and put down a saucer of milk for the White Cat. He was not to be found anywhere.

'I don't believe he came in at all last night,' the Little Dressmaker commented anxiously. 'I wonder where he is? I wonder if he has remembered we are going on a river picnic today?'

She wrote out a notice for him: GONE OUT. BACK LATER. SARDINES IN FRIDGE, and hung it round Dummy's neck on a piece of cotton. Ragdolly Anna took a last peep in the glass. Her hat looked beautiful, she thought. She had pressed the roses, gently, and even sewn on one or two new ones in places where they seemed a bit thin.

They picked up the baskets.

'Goodbye, Dummy. See you this evening,' they called. 'Don't get up to mischief.'

They were off.

At the bottom of the stairs, just by the street door, they turned, and looked up. They could see Dummy staring out of the window, with the 'almost smile' on her face and a notice about sardines round her neck. She would not get up to mischief. She was always good.

The bus came, red and comforting, after only a few minutes. When they scrambled on, Ragdolly Anna was pleased to find that downstairs was full up so that they had to go on top. It was much nicer on top, especially as the front seat was empty. It was directly over the engine, and rather bumpy. They could see splendidly.

Up this street and down that trundled the double-decker, past churches and schools and shops and recreation grounds and town halls and market stalls and offices. People got on, and bought their tickets, sat down and chatted, and got off again. The bell clanged. Gradually the shops and houses thinned out, and the streets turned into roads and the roads into lanes . . .

'It's the country,' explained the Little Dressmaker. 'Look – hay! Look – cows! Look – a farmhouse!'

Ragdolly Anna looked. She thought the cows were a bit frightening. They were so big. But they seemed gentle enough, quietly cropping the grass.

By the time they reached the end of their journey, the rest of the passengers had left. They came down the stairs carefully, holding on to the hand rail – and there, curled up in the place marked LUGGAGE, was the White Cat.

'A person must have some independence,' he told them, haughtily. '*Where* I got on . . . *How* I got on . . . *Why* I got on . . . is nothing to do with you. As it happens, I propose to fish.'

He arched his back and stretched. Beside him, neatly folded, was a fishing rod. And next to that, a tin that had once had tobacco in it.

'What's in the tin?' asked Ragdolly Anna.

'Bait.'

'What's bait?'

'Things to catch fish with, of course, stupid. Maggots.'

He opened the lid. Inside there was a crawling wriggling mass of yellowish-white maggots. 'See?'

Ragdolly Anna stepped back quickly. She did not like the maggots very much, and she was quite glad when the White Cat shouldered his fishing rod and walked off, proudly and stiffly, taking the maggots with him.

'You may not be aware,' he called over his tail, 'but I have become a member of the Anglers' Association, and I intend to make use of my rights.'

'What does he mean?' whispered Ragdolly Anna.

'He's just going to catch fish, that's all,' explained the Little Dressmaker, 'but he likes to be important.'

She paused, and closed her eyes dreamily.

'Smell!' she said.

Ragdolly Anna sniffed. There was a delicious smell. A smell of weeds and water lilies and minnows and wet wood and all sorts of exciting things she couldn't put a name to at all.

It was the river.

They picked up their baskets and walked down a path with a notice by it saying TO THE

BOATS. And there was the river itself. Ragdolly Anna had not imagined it would be so big or so beautiful. She had not guessed it would be moving gently all the time, as if it were going somewhere and was not to be put off on any account. All over the surface were crinkly marks and patterns. There were lilies, too, yellow ones with long writhing stalks like snakes, and round leaves like dinner plates. And underneath the water, if you looked down, you could see swarms of tiny fish as thin as pins, darting about together; and sometimes, a large, speckled one, thoughtful and lazy, lying still next to a stone – only the occasional movement of a fin told you that it was a fish at all.

The boats lay in a row, side by side, shifting and fidgeting. They were tied up so that they could not float away, and they *did* have cushions in them – just as the Little Dressmaker had said – and long poles, and paddles. They chose one with red cushions.

The boat wobbled a bit when they got in. Ragdolly Anna sat down quickly. She did not want to be upset. The Little Dressmaker said that poles were difficult. She was not very tall, and she thought she could manage a paddle better. She settled herself, right at the end of the punt. The boatman pushed them off . . . Ragdolly Anna lay back on the cushions, trailing her hand in the

water. It was refreshingly cool. They floated on, and on. The river turned and twisted. Round each corner there was a different view. 'Oh!' they cried, and 'Ah! Just look at that!' Sometimes they passed another punt going the other way, and then the Little Dressmaker kept close to the bank, for she did not want an accident. And once, a big steamer went by, churning up great waves into a 'wash'. Ragdolly Anna and the Little Dressmaker held on tight. Their punt went up and down quite violently – it was like riding on a rocking horse, and for a moment they felt a little sea-sick.

At midday they stopped for the picnic. An

overhanging willow made a good place to tie up the boat, and rather gingerly they stepped ashore, and took out the baskets.

They were hungry. It seemed *ages* since breakfast, and they made short work of the sandwiches and biscuits. Ragdolly Anna drank lemonade out of a bottle. It was more difficult than she had imagined ... she made glug-glug noises, and dribbled, until she got into the way of it. The Little Dressmaker had a hot drink and then decided to take a nap. It was a pity that the grass was damp. They spread some of the picnic paper on it, and she lay down carefully so as not to spoil her dress, and shut her eyes ...

A dragonfly darted over the water, to and fro, to and fro, royal blue and glittering. Ragdolly Anna thought she would like to try fishing. As quietly as she could, she crept to the bank, taking the jam jars with her.

The Little Dressmaker heard movements, and opened one eye. 'You have to lower the jar into the water,' she explained sleepily, 'and wait till a fish swims over the top. Then pull it up.'

She drifted into sleep again, and a butterfly settled for a moment on her cheek.

Ragdolly Anna lowered both the jam jars, and waited. She waited a long time. Eventually a shoal of minnows swam briskly over the jars, and pulling them up with a jerk she found that she had caught three. They weren't very big. 'About as big as safety pins,' she thought, and stared at them closely. They kept pushing at the glass with their noses, as if they didn't like being caught, so she soon tipped them back, and tried again. It wasn't so easy then. But further out, towards the middle of the stream, a fine, dark, mud-coloured fish floated steadily, waving his fins . . .

'I wish I could get *him*!' Ragdolly Anna stretched herself on her tummy. She had tucked her dress into her bloomers so that it would not get wet, and she reached out with a jam jar as far as she possibly could – further . . . and further . . . and a bit further.

Suddenly – *flip*! A branch from the willow tree overhead caught the brim of her hat and tipped it neatly into the water . . .

'OH!' cried Ragdolly Anna. 'My hat! It's gone! QUICK!'

She jumped up and ran along the bank. The hat was floating downstream quite fast, turning round and round in circles as it went. It was certainly out of reach. The Little Dressmaker had woken with a start, and immediately began piling the picnic things back into the punt. She untied the rope, and Ragdolly Anna pushed off and scrambled in. She was almost crying. She wished she could manage to use a paddle, too;

but she wasn't big enough. It seemed a dreadfully long time before they got the punt into midstream, and made their way with a great deal of splashing and panting after the hat. It looked like a water lily ... a water lily that wouldn't keep still. On and on, round and round, it went, and the Little Dressmaker got quite hot and flustered, trying to catch up with it. But however hard she paddled, it was always just out of reach.

Soon they came to a noticeboard saying DANGER, in capital letters, NO BOATS BEYOND THIS POINT. It must be the weir.

Resting for a moment, they listened. There was a roaring, rushing sound, like a hundred tigers. Ragdolly Anna burst into tears. It was a good thing she had remembered to bring a clean handkerchief with her. They drew into the bank, and stopped to think what they should do next. A few yards away somebody was fishing. Through her tears Ragdolly Anna watched, as he twirled the line round his head, and cast beautifully, right into the centre of the stream. Surely she knew that figure? Yes! It was the White Cat.

Maybe he could help.

She scrambled to her feet, and waved. The White Cat listened sympathetically as she told her story, hiccupping every now and then so that

48

it was sometimes hard for him to understand what she was saying.

'Hat in the stream?' he questioned. 'A most unfortunate occurrence, certainly. But I think we can soon settle that little problem. I think we can!'

Swiftly he trotted along the edge of the river, taking his rod with him, till he was exactly opposite Ragdolly Anna's hat. You could see that the paper roses were getting wet, but it was still floating quite merrily on the surface, though it was dangerously close to the weir. Ragdolly Anna shuddered. The water made a great noise, crashing and swooshing. It was frightening.

There was no time to waste. The White Cat stood firmly on his hind legs, and twirled the line three times round his head. There was a hook on the end of it. The first time it came down several inches short of the hat; the second time, it was too far on the other side. At the *third* throw the hook caught on the straw, the hat was neatly twitched out of the water, and came flying safely ashore.

Saved!

They shook it, and smoothed it, and laid it gently in the sun to dry.

'It's extremely fortunate that we happened to see you,' commented the Little Dressmaker. 'Otherwise we should have lost the hat for ever. It would have disappeared in the weir.'

'A little experience ... a little knowledge ... it's what we call "know-how",' said the White Cat, modestly. 'Don't mention it. We cannot *all* have the skill for fishing hats. It's an art. But of course we cats are a talented race. Everybody knows *that*.'

Later that afternoon, sitting on the bus, all three of them in a row, they felt strangely different from the rest of the passengers. They were damp, and tousled, and had grass in their hair. Ragdolly Anna's hat was a little bedraggled and her bloomers had mud on them. There was also a strong smell of fresh fish, for in his bag the White Cat had two fine trout which they would have for supper. Anyone could tell they had spent a day on the river.

At home, five flights up, Dummy was waiting for them by the window. She was in exactly the same position as she had been when they had left. The notice about sardines hung round her neck, and she had her 'almost smile' on her face as if she had been enjoying herself too.

'Have *you* had a good day?' whispered Ragdolly Anna, throwing her arms round Dummy's neck and giving her a hug. Dummy did not answer. But in the middle of her delicately drawn mouth there seemed to float a little sound.

It *might* have been

'Yes!'

Ragdolly Anna
at the Museum

*

It was on Ragdolly Anna's birthday that the Little Dressmaker started talking about museums.

'They are places,' she explained, 'where you can go and look at things which are special. Specially old, perhaps, or specially beautiful. Would you like to go? It would be a treat. You can wear your new dress.'

Ragdolly Anna clapped her hands. The trouble about having a winter birthday was that it was never any good for picnics. You couldn't spend a day on the river when it was pouring with sleet. You couldn't have a garden party – even if you had a garden – or a trip to the swings in the park. But a museum! That would be something different.

The White Cat yawned, and stretched his claws. He surveyed them, critically. 'If you want Education,' he said haughtily, 'come to me. For a small remuneration, I would consider a course of instruction. It's no good going to museums if you don't know *anything*.' He sniffed.

'What's a "remuneration"?' whispered Ragdolly Anna to the Little Dressmaker.

'He means he wants to be paid. I expect a halfpenny would do. I found a halfpenny under the gas stove this morning. Give him that.'

'Thank you!' said Ragdolly Anna. She took the halfpenny and polished it with her handkerchief, and the White Cat received it graciously and put it away under his cushion. He was saving up for a new fishing rod.

'We shall begin with the Stone Age,' he mewed. 'You would be wise to take down the facts in your notebook. That is what notebooks are for.'

Ragdolly Anna liked writing things down. She wrote STONE AGE in capital letters, and listened ... The White Cat seemed to know a great deal. He went on and on, in a high pitched mew, telling about cooking pots and food and fires and caves and tools and clothes and climate. Sometimes he cleared his throat. Always he looked important. It was nearly dinner-time before he had finished. The Little Dressmaker thought if he didn't soon stop they would never get to the museum at all.

'We must hurry,' she said, dishing up a treacle

roly-poly. 'We'll go on the tube – it will be quicker.'

They ate so fast that Ragdolly Anna burnt her tongue a bit on the treacle, but she didn't like to mention it. In five minutes they were ready. Dummy and the White Cat watched them go.

Ragdolly Anna wasn't fond of the underground. She didn't like the darkness, and she didn't like the noise, and the smell was dreadful; but once you got used to it it was really interesting to follow the map on the wall and see where you were going. They stopped quite near the museum.

The doors were ENORMOUS. She felt very

small going up the steps, but the Little Dress-maker held her hand. Inside was a new world. Directions pointed here, and there: to the Turkish treasures and to the Chinese jade; to the Indian canoes and the Japanese embroideries. They hurried down this hallway and up that. Ragdolly Anna stared and stared. When they came to the Stone Age section she was glad she had listened to the White Cat. After all, you never knew when Education might be useful.

There was one case which had a peculiarly shaped bone in it. It almost seemed to have a head and a body. Could it be a Stone Age doll?

Ragdolly Anna stood by that case for a long time.

'If you don't mind, love,' whispered the Little Dressmaker, 'I'll go on to the Egyptians. You stay here. Your legs aren't so long as mine. Don't move – then I'll know where to find you. I'll not be long.'

She trotted down the gallery and disappeared.

'When you are on your own,' said Ragdolly Anna to herself firmly, 'it is best to keep still. Then you don't get lost.'

So she kept still. She didn't even flutter an eyelash.

Soon she began to be noticed.

''Ere, 'Arry! What's this?' called a voice.

'It's a doll, isn't it?'

'What's it doing there?'

'Must have fallen out of one of the cases . . .'

'Somebody ought to be *told* about it . . .'

'Somebody ought to put it back.'

Then a different sort of voice broke in: 'Doesn't look like a Stone Age doll to *me*! They wouldn't have hats in those days. Not with roses on, anyway.' An old man with a thick muffler round his neck and a red handkerchief in his pocket looked kindly down at Ragdolly Anna. Quite a big crowd had gathered round. She did not very much like being called IT.

'But I'd better not speak,' she thought. 'I'd better pretend to be a Stone Age doll, and not answer at all. I must be as stiff as a fireguard . . . then no one will guess . . .'

'Out of my way, please,' ordered a museum attendant. 'Kindly do not touch the exhibits. That doll should never have been removed from the case.' He hurried up. 'Excuse me! Thank you.' He took a key from his pocket, and without more than a brief glance at Ragdolly Anna, he picked her up and popped her inside the exhibition case! He locked it, carefully, and went away.

'It doesn't seem right to me,' muttered the old man with the red handkerchief. 'It doesn't *look* like a Stone Age doll. Where would they have got the roses? It bothers me.' He had a pleasant voice, and he sounded anxious.

Nobody answered him. Gradually, the crowd began to move off.

'I'm *not* a museum piece at all!' whispered Ragdolly Anna. She was feeling frightened.

The old man turned round. 'What did you say?'

'I don't belong here! I don't! I belong to the Little Dressmaker. Let me out! Oh, *please* let me out!'

Ragdolly Anna did not like being in a glass case. Well – would *you*? It was stuffy, and dusty, and she couldn't open the windows. She banged on the glass with her fists, but it wasn't any use. The bone doll did not speak at all. 'I expect it's had no Education,' thought Ragdolly Anna. 'I do wish I could get out,' she repeated aloud, struggling with the lock and the handle.

The old man really seemed to be taking some notice of her. His eyes opened wider and wider. 'God bless my soul! So you are a *real* young lady!'

'I'm as real as you,' insisted Ragdolly Anna. 'Let me out, *please*!'

'Well, I could ask the attendant to unlock the case, but he thinks you belong to the museum.'

He leaned forward and pressed his nose against the glass. 'Tell you what, though. I've got a *special* key of my own that might do the trick. I don't say it *will*, mind – you never know for certain. But it might. Let's have a try.'

He took off his overcoat. Underneath he wore a jacket and a pullover; and underneath the pullover was a waistcoat with a chain. You could see the chain dangling beneath the bottom button. On it hung a tiny, glittering key.

'See this?' The old man unhooked it carefully. 'There's not another key like this anywhere. It's magic. Sometimes it opens things; sometimes it doesn't. It all depends on the what and the wherefore. Had it for seventeen years, I have. Older than you, it must be, by a long shot. Eh?'

'*Much* older,' agreed Ragdolly Anna, trying not to sound impatient. She watched.

Delicately the old man inserted the key in the lock. Delicately, very gently, so as to be sure not to break anything, he turned it . . .

There was a click.

'There! What did I say? It's worked.' He opened the door wide, and lifted Ragdolly Anna out. She sighed with relief. Then he closed it, being particularly careful to fasten the lock again exactly as it was before.

It was important that the bone doll should be safe. After all, she *did* belong there. It was her home.

'Rescued! *Now* what am I going to do with you?'

'If you could direct me to the Egyptian department,' begged Ragdolly Anna, when she had thanked him, 'I shall find the Little Dressmaker. Because that's where she said she was going to be.'

They set off for the Egyptian department in good spirits. Ragdolly Anna held the old man's sleeve. She peeped up at him. He had such a kind face. His cheeks were rosy, like red peppers, and his hair was curly and white. He reminded her of someone. Who? Could it be Father Christmas?

'Are you,' she asked, 'Father Chr . . .?'

The old man laughed. 'You're wrong,' he answered. 'I'm not Father Christmas. He lives at the North Pole; it's too cold for me there. And such a lot of correspondence. But he *is* a relation of mine. I'm his cousin. People often tell me there is a likeness. Mind you, he wears a scarlet hood, and combinations. I don't. I prefer a cap, myself, and muffler. But a hood keeps your ears warm and that's very necessary in the land of ice and snow. And combinations. Here we are.'

The Egyptian department was splendid. There were cases full of jewels, masks, and ornaments. There were gold cups and plates, and jugs with such beautiful decorations that Ragdolly Anna wondered how anyone could bear to put anything in them. At the end of the gallery were some large stone carvings: a strange sort of creature called a sphinx, a bird, a snake . . . a sitting cat. The cat held itself very upright, looking exactly ahead of it, with its tail curled round its paws.

The Little Dressmaker was standing by it. She turned to welcome Ragdolly Anna. 'Oh, *there* you are. I was just coming. It was kind of you to bring her to me, Mister –' But Father Christmas's cousin had disappeared. He just wasn't there.

'It's very odd,' commented Ragdolly Anna. 'Where *is* he? He was looking after me. He was so nice. I thought he could come home and have tea with us. And now he's gone.'

'Never mind!' The Little Dressmaker comforted her. 'We may meet him again some day. We must look out for him. I'll ask Dummy to be on

the watch. She's always gazing out of the window. I do believe she can see things that nobody else can see ... and maybe Father Christmas's cousin will be one of them.'

There was a sort of mew from the stone cat.

'If you require information,' it announced in a hoarse mumble, hardly moving its lips at all, 'look up *People of Importance*, under C. You will find Christmas (Father), and Christmas (Cousin). You will also find Cat (White). That's me, naturally. Didn't recognize me, did you?'

Ragdolly Anna jumped. 'What are *you* doing?' she asked. 'I thought you were a statue.'

'In ancient times,' explained the White Cat, 'I was worshipped. Cats were considered to be MORE IMPORTANT THAN ANYTHING ELSE. Well, of course, we all know that's true, but not everybody remembers it. I frequently spend an afternoon in the Egyptian department. People come to admire me. Very right and proper. I'll be home later. At supper-time.' He closed one eye.

'We'd better leave him,' murmured the Little Dressmaker. 'Look. There's a guide coming, and a lot more visitors. He *will* be pleased. Let's go home and have tea.'

'Will it be a Birthday Tea?' asked Ragdolly Anna. She skipped after the Little Dressmaker, as they made their way through corridors and down staircases and up *more* staircases and round corners, until they came to the great doors and the street.

It was already dusk. The underground train looked like a dragon, with gleaming eyes, as it roared out of the tunnel ... *WHOOSH*!

'Of *course* it will be a Birthday Tea,' answered the Little Dressmaker as soon as she had got her breath back. She put the tickets she was holding into her handbag, and fastened it with a snap. 'I've made a cake. With candles on.'

'How many?' asked Ragdolly Anna excitedly.

'Ah! That I'm not telling. It's to be a surprise. Guess!'

Ragdolly Anna started to count. She was not very good at counting, especially when she was in an underground train. The noise put her off.

After a little while, she gave up trying.

'I'll ask Dummy, when we get home,' she decided drowsily. '*She'll* know how old I am. But I wonder if she'll tell?'

Ragdolly Anna
Goes to the Fair

*

'What's this?' Ragdolly Anna held up something round, silvery, and small which she had discovered by the corner of the skirting board.

'It's a five-pence piece. It must have fallen out of my jacket pocket,' answered the Little Dressmaker. 'I *thought* I had a hole. See if you can mend it for me, there's a love.' She spoke in a screwed-up sort of voice, because she was fitting Dummy with a lace bodice, and carried pins in the corner of her mouth. Ragdolly Anna was learning to sew, and was quite good at simple bits of mending; but she was never allowed to carry pins in her mouth in case she swallowed them.

She found the jacket. Yes, there *was* a hole in the pocket, so she dragged it over to the bed and spread it out. Then she sat herself on the pillow and began to stitch up the gap ...

'I ought to *know* about money,' she said. 'I ought to know which are the brown ones, and which are the silvery ones, and which are the paper ones, and which are the ones with sides and corners. I ought to be able to count properly, and add up . . .'

'Counting,' the Little Dressmaker assured her, 'is easy. You could learn quickly, if I lent you my button box. Multiplication and division are harder. But if you were to do a little arithmetic every morning, you'd soon pick it up. We must see what can be done.'

She stuck a final pin in the bodice, and drew it over Dummy's head very, very gently, so that it didn't fall to bits. 'We'll start tomorrow,' she decided.

Ragdolly Anna was excited. In the evening, while the Little Dressmaker was making scrambled eggs for supper, she talked to Dummy. Dummy was always a good listener. She never interrupted, and she never disapproved of what you told her you were going to do. She always looked a little past you – not straight at you, of course, because that might make you feel shy – but over your shoulder; and she always had a half-smile on her face.

'I'm going to borrow the button box,' whispered Ragdolly Anna. She put both hands up to her hat, and pulled it down, firmly. 'I'm going to learn to do sums, so that I'll know how to spend my five-pence piece.'

The Little Dressmaker had allowed Ragdolly Anna to keep the five-pence piece. She had made her a tiny purse, and had sewn a pocket inside her velvet cloak to keep the purse in so that it would not get lost.

In the morning they got out the button box and arranged the buttons in piles, and heaps, and patterns. They were fascinating buttons, and each of them had a story attached to it. It was quite hard to concentrate on taking away nine buttons from ten, without remembering that the tenth one had been left over from the wedding dress of the lady who kept the wool shop. And the

ninth button had come off Tommy Biddle's trousers. And the eighth was an overcoat button they had found on the bus. And so on. But Ragdolly Anna tried hard; she *was* a little bit clever, although she was only made of cloth pieces, and she soon learned all her tables and could even say some of them backwards.

'Twice eleven is twenty-two, twice twelve is twenty-four,' she told the White Cat. He sat on the window-sill, thoughtfully curling his claws and uncurling them again. Now and then he sharpened them on the furniture.

'Who cares?' scoffed the White Cat, haughtily. 'Huh!'

Dummy said nothing at all. She couldn't manage numbers, and the Little Dressmaker warned that she was not to be troubled with them. They might make her sick, and then what would they do? 'We all have our places in the world,' she explained, 'and not everyone feels comfortable with mathematics.'

After a week or two Ragdolly Anna had learned so much that she began to keep housekeeping accounts. The Little Dressmaker made her a special accounts book out of the backs of old envelopes fastened together with a safety pin, and she wrote down:

'brussel sprouts, 30p
carrots, 8p
oranges, three for 20p
potatoes, 28p'

Then she added it all up, so they knew what had happened to the money when it wasn't there any more. There wasn't *much* money, to be sure. The Little Dressmaker worked from early in the morning until late at night, but she was not very good at sending in bills: and even when she *did* manage to write one out properly and put it in an envelope and address it and stick a stamp on, she only charged a small amount for even the most elaborate dresses.

'Never mind,' comforted Ragdolly Anna, when they had to give up the Sunday joint because sausages were cheaper. 'I *like* sausages.' She did, too. She liked the tiny ones with no skins on.

One Friday evening, when the Little Dressmaker was finishing her work and putting it tidily away, she paused for a moment . . .

'Listen!'

They listened. There was a faint, very faint, sound of music. Not television music, or radio music, or transistor music, but music that seemed exciting, and alive.

It sounded like an organ. Not a church organ, either, but one of those that you sometimes find

68

in the middle of a whirling roundabout. There is a huge handle to it, and a man has to turn the handle, and out comes a tune – colourful, loud, merry – the sort of tune you feel you have to dance to, even if you are eighty-seven and have a wooden leg.

'It's the Fair,' cried the Little Dressmaker. She clasped her hands together. 'I do love a Fair. We must go!'

'*All* of us?' asked Ragdolly Anna, excitedly.

'Not Dummy. She wouldn't like it. There'd be too many people, and she's never happy in crowds. And not the White Cat – he doesn't care about such things. But you and I, Ragdolly Anna. We'll go tonight!'

The Little Dressmaker looked in the house-keeping purse to see how much money there was to spare ...

There wasn't much. Only a fifty-pence piece and a few pennies. But she remembered an old jam jar she kept for halfpennies – and sure enough, there were forty-three halfpennies in it, which comes to quite a lot if you add it up carefully.

'And here's my five-pence,' said Ragdolly Anna.

They went down the five flights of stairs feeling quite rich. They didn't seem to care that the lift wasn't working again.

Outside it was crisp and chilly. Ragdolly Anna was glad she was wearing her velvet cloak. The Fair was pitched in a nearby recreation ground. You could find your way easily by following the music. It grew louder, and louder, and louder. Then suddenly they were in the midst of everything.

Swingboats, coconut shies, helter-skelter, apple-dipping, penny-rolling, darts ... Was there anything that wasn't there? Dodgem cars crashed into one another, and people screamed and shouted. The Little Dressmaker didn't much care for those. But she stood for a long while by the Hoop-la stall. There were so many odds and ends which she thought she might like – a bit of scented soap, for example, which would be a luxury for special occasions; a pair of rubber gloves for washing up; a pack of cards to pass the dark winter evenings; a bracelet; a necklace of coloured beads. She spent five-pence on three quoits. She threw one, and then another ...

No luck.

'Let me try,' begged Ragdolly Anna.

'I've only one left – don't *waste* it,' said the Little Dressmaker. 'You have to aim. I wonder if you are tall enough?'

Ragdolly Anna stretched herself as tall as she could. It wasn't easy, and the quoit was so big she had to hold it with both hands. Maybe if she

70

balanced on top of a tent peg? She shut her eyes, after that, and held her breath, and threw it up in the air as high as it would go.

Then she stood still, not daring to look.

'We've won! We've won, Ragdolly Anna!' called the Little Dressmaker excitedly. 'It's fallen on the coloured bead necklace, *exactly*!'

It was true. The quoit had come down plump in the middle of the table, and the necklace was plump in the middle of the quoit. Trembling, Ragdolly Anna looked at it. '*You* have it,' she said.

'But *you* won it,' argued the Little Dressmaker. She held the necklace in her hand, and fondled it lovingly. There were a great many tiny beads – hundreds and hundreds of them. Could it be possible that it might be divided into two? Ragdolly Anna would only want a short one.

'That's what we'll do when we get home,' she decided. 'I'll snip it, very carefully, and make one long necklace and one short one. Then we shall *both* have a prize!' They walked on. They were fortunate with the coconuts, and got one with their first try. It was just luck, the Little Dressmaker thought, but Ragdolly Anna believed it was because the gentleman next to her had jogged her elbow.

At last it grew dusk. Lights twinkled on every stall. They went on the helter-skelter, and the

Little Dressmaker turned rather pale at the speed of it. They had a go on the swing-boats, and Ragdolly Anna felt quite dreamy with the sway of them. The roundabout they saved till the end. There wasn't much money left, by then – with Ragdolly Anna's five-pence piece it was just enough for one ride. Louder and louder sounded the music, faster and faster went the roundabout horses. Some were black, some dappled, some grey, but they all had tossing manes that reminded Ragdolly Anna of the big fluffs of candyfloss you could buy to lick. Their eyes were staring, their black hooves shone . . .

She looked and looked, undecided which one to choose.

They slowed to a standstill.

'I don't want a go, love,' said the Little Dressmaker. 'It's too fast for me. *You* go, and I'll wait here for you. Hold on tight, mind, and be careful not to let your hat blow off.'

Ragdolly Anna climbed on to the black horse with a green saddle. She had been watching him. She felt sure that there was something about him which was a bit different from the others.

He *was* different from the others, too, for suddenly he began to speak, and proper language, at that!

'You ever seen a Night Mare?'

Ragdolly Anna nodded. She had had a nightmare once. It was after they had eaten toasted cheese for supper, and then meringues and ice-cream, for a birthday celebration. She had felt hot and cold and horrible in the middle of the night, and had sat up, suddenly sobbing because she had dreamed she was being toasted under the grill with the cheese. 'It is a nightmare,' the Little Dressmaker had said, comfortingly. 'You must have eaten too much. Turn over on the other side and think of Christmas.' And so she had. Nightmares were unpleasant. She knew that.

'I am the Night Mare's good brother,' went on

the roundabout horse. 'Night Mare is in charge of the bad dreams. I am in charge of the good ones. I keep them in my saddle. It is rather a peculiar shape – perhaps you have noticed?'

Ragdolly Anna *had* noticed that there was a sort of egg-shaped hump on the front of the saddle, with a lock on it. She had wondered what it was for.

'Would you like a dream?' asked the round-about horse. They were whirling round at such a rate she could hardly hear the question, and she certainly could not shout loudly enough to answer him, so she nodded her head violently and mouthed 'Yes, please!' and waited for what was going to happen next.

'Look in my left ear, and you will find a key.'

Ragdolly Anna leaned forward. It was true. Inside the roundabout horse's left ear was a small, gold key.

'Quick, now. Unlock the saddle box, help yourself, lock it up again and replace the key in my left ear.'

Ragdolly Anna did as she was told. At first, it was quite difficult to fit the key in the lock be-cause it was so tiny, and, after all, they were still going up and down, and round and round, but at last she managed it; and sure enough, inside the saddle box were seven little parcels, one for each night of the week, pink, blue, green, yellow, red, orange, and purple.

Which should she choose?

After a moment's hesitation, she picked up the pink one. It was as soft and silky as a feather.

'Swallow it!' whispered the Dream Horse.

A little doubtfully, she put it in on the end of her tongue. It was sweet – not at all nasty – and reminded her of pear drops.

In a second, it was gone.

The roundabout had stopped. There stood the Little Dressmaker, waiting for her. Some of the stalls were already closing. It was time to go home.

'Goodbye, Dream Horse,' said Ragdolly Anna. 'Thank you for the dream!' She stroked his mane, and slid to the ground.

'We must hurry.' The Little Dressmaker didn't like going to bed too late, and was anxious to get home.

Tired, but happy, they made their way through the thinning crowds, out of the recreation ground, up this street and down that, till they came to the flats. And there, high up, five floors above them, they could just see the White Cat looking out of the window in a disapproving way.

'Ought to have been home *ages* ago,' he chided as they came to the door. 'What about my milk?'

76

Ragdolly Anna poured some into a saucer. The White Cat took some time, lapping it up. 'And I *don't* want to hear about the Fair,' he mewed huffily.

'Never mind. Dummy will be interested,' replied Ragdolly Anna.

While the Little Dressmaker was cleaning her teeth, four times upwards and four times down, and putting her hair in curlers ready for bed, Ragdolly Anna sat on a cushion and told Dummy all that had happened to them. 'You can have a bit of the necklace, if you like,' she promised kindly, 'because you couldn't go to the Fair.'

Dummy looked past her stiffly. She didn't say a word, but she seemed pleased.

'I wonder if I *shall* dream tonight?' thought Ragdolly Anna. She put her hat carefully away in its box, and folded up her clothes. She stood her shoes side by side, ready for the morning. She clambered into bed, and shut her eyes . . .

The room seemed to be full of bright pink roundabout horses, galloping round and round, and up and up and down and down, slipping into darkness and out again. Ragdolly Anna was fast asleep, dreaming the dream the roundabout horse had promised her.

Ragdolly Anna
Goes Sledging

*

Ragdolly Anna felt there was something peculiar as soon as she opened her eyes. It was her nose that told her. It was not warm and comfortable, as it usually was, but cold – very cold – and as sharp as a clothes peg. She rubbed it.

The Little Dressmaker was already up, and making a cup of tea. She seemed worried.

'Look at the windows!' she exclaimed. 'We can't see out at all! They're frosted over. And I had a terrible job getting the curtains back – they were frozen to the pane. Something must have happened to the heating. The pipes are quite cold.' She had pinned a blanket round her shoulders, and as Ragdolly Anna was dressing she insisted that she should wear two of everything in case she caught pneumonia. 'And remember,' she said, 'pneumonia begins with a p.'

The White Cat was curled up on a cushion, with his tail over his toes. 'Here I am,' he mumbled, 'and here I shall stay until things are right again. It's my belief that there has been snow in the night. I can smell it.'

Ragdolly Anna ran to the window. The panes were so thickly furred with frost that you couldn't see what was happening outside at all; the pictures on the glass were beautiful. They were of enchanted forests and dragons and lakes and mountains, shells, stars, and patterns; they shone and twinkled like diamonds.

Ragdolly Anna made her mouth into an O, and breathed.

A round hole came into the middle of the forest, and through it she could peer down, down, down, five flights of stairs into the street.

It didn't look like a street any more. It was white, and clean, and as fresh as new bread. You might have guessed that nobody was about at all, except that across the whiteness were one or two dark squiggles and blodges where the newspaper boy and the postman had trudged, and left footprints.

'Whatever shall we do?' wailed the Little Dressmaker. 'I promised to deliver a winter cloak with a fur collar on it, this morning. The snow's quite thick. The buses won't be running. And it's *much* too deep for me to walk.'

She wiped her eyes on the edge of the blanket.

'We must *bang* the pipes, so that the water comes through. Perhaps they are frozen.'

So they banged. The Little Dressmaker banged quite hard, with a wooden spatula. Ragdolly Anna banged with a teaspoon. Before long, there was a gurgle ... a whistle ... a plop ... gradually the pipes began to warm up. Dummy was wearing the winter cloak with the fur collar. She had been wound very thin, because it was for a thin person, and when the Little Dressmaker had taken the cloak off and packed it in a cardboard box with layers and layers of tissue paper, she threw a silk cloth over her to keep off the draughts. Ragdolly Anna *thought* she heard Dummy sneeze – just a tiny, faint whuffle, like a piece of thistledown drifting away, but she couldn't be certain.

Gradually the windows cleared. When they had made the bed, and watered the bulb bowls, they looked out again. The sky was strangely misted. A few soft flakes floated gently down, and then more, and more and more. They grew quite dazed, staring at them.

'It's a good job we *are* five floors up,' thought Ragdolly Anna. 'Or we'd be buried.'

Soon a boy went by with a sledge. And then a group of children, running and shouting. There was the thud of snowballs, and someone fell over and bumped his nose and cried; but he was quickly dragged up again and hustled off with the others, leaving a dark, ragged gash in the smooth snow behind him.

'I wish I had a sledge,' mused Ragdolly Anna.

'If I *can't* deliver the parcel,' worried the Little Dressmaker, 'I shall lose a good customer. And she'll want to wear her cloak in this weather. She'll be miserable without it. What *is* to be done?'

'Send Ragdolly Anna,' advised the White Cat, sleepily. 'She's got gumboots. I haven't.'

'She's not big enough. It's a very *big* parcel. And I don't like her to run errands on her own.'

'Tell her to take a sledge.' He yawned, and washed his whiskers delicately with a white paw. 'That'd be safe enough. Put the parcel on the sledge. And let her pull it.'

'We haven't *got* a sledge,' sighed the Little Dressmaker regretfully. 'We had one, once, but it went to a rummage sale by mistake. It never came back.'

'Such stupidity!' scoffed the White Cat. He stretched, and arched his back. 'Use a tea tray, then. I'm off. I'm going to rest myself in the airing cupboard. Imagination, that's what you need. And enterprise.'

He stalked off with his tail in the air, and settled down between the sheets and towels. It was a lovely place to spend the winter. He purred.

'It's an idea, certainly. There *is* an old tea tray in the back of the larder. A tin one,' said the Little Dressmaker thoughtfully. 'But do you think you could possibly manage? I could write down the address, and tie it round your neck.'

'Of *course* I could,' burst out Ragdolly Anna.

'You'd have to go straight there and back, mind. No dawdling.'

They rummaged about under the shelves at the back of the larder, disturbing two beetles and a large spider, who scuttled away angrily. And there was the tray. It was a red tin one, quite large. The parcel would fit it perfectly; the Little Dressmaker stuck it on firmly with Sellotape, and made a pulling rope out of a bit of clothes line. Then she helped Ragdolly Anna get ready. She had such a lot of clothes to wear, she could hardly move. The Little Dressmaker tied her hat on with a huge woollen scarf that went over and under and round, so that it kept her neck warm as well. There wasn't much left of Ragdolly Anna herself to be seen. Luckily the lift was working properly, so it was quite easy for Ragdolly Anna to get the sledge and the parcel down five flights to the ground floor, and out of the front door. She looked up, and waved.

At first, the brightness quite hurt her eyes. The

snow was quite deep, and would have gone into her gumboots, but fortunately she wasn't heavy – for she was only made of rags – so she ran lightly over the top of it, and the tray slithered along behind, exactly like a real sledge.

Getting there was easy enough. She panted a bit as she dragged the parcel up three steps to a big front door, and knocked. A lady opened it. It was embarrassing, being a rag doll, and not quite a human being, so she didn't stay, once she had presented the parcel.

But it was more difficult going back. The snow had covered her footmarks, she was beginning to feel cold, and her nose wanted blowing. She was

tired. She couldn't reach her handkerchief inside all those layers, so she wiped her nose on her sleeve, and trudged on, pulling the tea tray behind her. 'It is so hard to remember the way with all this snow about,' thought Ragdolly Anna. 'I ought to have dropped crumbs to mark the track.'

It was only when she had been going for at least three quarters of an hour, and saw some long, snow-covered barges a few yards off, that she realized she wasn't on the road at all, but on the canal. It was frozen.

She was lost. Far ahead stretched the canal, into a white, mysterious distance. She might never, never get home again. Every familiar landmark had disappeared, or turned into something different.

Ragdolly Anna stopped dead. 'I mustn't cry,' she told herself. 'I must be sensible. I must think of the people climbing Mount Everest. The question is, what to do next?'

'It's *always* the question,' answered a drowsy voice from behind one of the barges. It sounded as if it came from somebody with his mouth full. 'And there's always an answer. Not everybody can find it, mind you. But not everybody wants to know. First of all, you have to decide whether it is to be *forward*, or *back*. That's important. It's not all that difficult,' went on the voice, in a muffled sort of way. 'I've done it often, myself. So I know. I'm always at it. I come and I go.'

A horse was tethered to a barge that seemed a little different from the others. It had curtains, and there was a tiny garden. You could see flower-pots poking out of the snow. The horse was eating hay, and talking at the same time. Long wisps hung out of the sides of his mouth. Ragdolly Anna hadn't met many horses – you don't, if you live in a flat five floors up – but this one seemed kindly, and she was glad of a little conversation, even if it *did* seem rather peculiar.

'But if I don't know where I am, how do I know which way to go?'

'This way – Birmingham. That way – London,' answered the barge horse. 'Where do you *want* to go? That's the problem. Just answer that – if you can. You've got to have a destination.'

'I want to go home,' said Ragdolly Anna. She sniffed.

'Ah! In that case, my master might be able to help you. He's a great one for giving directions. A *great* one, *he* is. Neigh!' He curled his upper lip so that he almost looked as if he were smiling, and rubbed the barge window with a swish of his tail.

A face looked out.

What a face! It had a long beard, and wispy hair, and the bluest eyes Ragdolly Anna had ever seen.

85

'She wants to go home,' explained the barge horse.

The face raised its eyebrows. 'Why not?' it asked. The eyes narrowed; then they opened again, and began to twinkle. 'It's Ragdolly Anna, isn't it? What are *you* doing on the canal on a winter's morning? Time you were back, five floors up, with a hot water bottle. But I can't move me boat till the ice melts. Old Horse'll take you. I'll give him directions. A good friend to me, was the Little Dressmaker. I remember her, I do. Made me an eiderdown out of ducks' feathers, she did. Tell her I haven't forgot. It's the warmest eiderdown I've ever had. Bob the Bargee's my name – she's sure to call it to mind.'

Bob the Bargee appeared on deck. He was wearing mittens, but he was clever with his hands, although they were gnarled and lumpy. He tied the tray rope on to Old Horse's harness, and knotted it with a special sort of knot that wouldn't come undone.

'Now. *You* sit on the tray. That's it! All right? Hold on tight – we don't want any accidents.'

He turned back to the barge.

'Like a hot sausage roll to keep your hands warm? You would?'

'Please!' said Ragdolly Anna. It was long past dinner-time. She was feeling really hungry.

'Heave ho, then!' He nipped down a ladder,

and was up again in no time with a hot sausage
roll in his fingers. 'Now, listen, old fellow.
You take the first right, second left, carry on
over the traffic lights, past the playing fields,
left again at the ironmonger what sells fish hooks,
right again, straight on, under the subway, cross
the road opposite the Palladium, and Bob's your
uncle!'

He grinned. 'Heave ho! Haul up the anchor,
and off yer goes.' With a slap and a whistle, they
were away.

It was exciting, being pulled along the frozen
canal. Ragdolly Anna felt like somebody in a
fairy tale, only there weren't any fairies. She

snuggled down into her scarf, and nibbled the sausage roll. It *did* keep her hands warm, and she made it last as long as possible. Then, gradually, they drew near the town. They passed the traffic lights, the playing fields, the ironmonger's; they went under the subway, across the road – and there were the flats where the Little Dressmaker and Dummy and the White Cat were impatiently waiting for her.

It was the White Cat who first saw the pair of them approaching, and loped downstairs to meet them. 'Some people,' he complained severely, 'have *no* thought for others. You've been *ages*. Why on earth didn't you mark the way? Sheer carelessness. *She* thought you had been buried in the snow, but *I* didn't. Decent of the horse to bring you. Would he like some milk?'

The barge horse refused, politely; he helped Ragdolly Anna untie the tray, and turned to go.

'Always glad to be of use,' he said mildly. 'It was just a matter of following directions.'

'You and I can understand such things, old fellow,' said the White Cat loftily. 'But *she* can't. She's not an animal, you know. She's not even human. However – goodbye. *Au revoir*,' he added, to show that he knew another language. 'I may see you some time.' He stepped elegantly up the stairs, with Ragdolly Anna, to the fifth floor.

Dummy was wearing an old stocking round

her throat, because it was a little sore. She had been wound out and out and out, so that she was really fat and comfortable, and had been partly fitted with a red flannel petticoat.

'It *was* kind of you to do my errand, love,' said the Little Dressmaker. 'But I *was* anxious. Yes, I remember Bob the Bargee. He gave me a bucket with flowers painted on it. He was so grateful for that eiderdown.'

Ragdolly Anna had saved a bit of snow to keep for ever. She had put it in her purse.

But when she unfastened the clip to show it to the White Cat, there was nothing in it at all. It was quite empty, but rather damp.

'I suppose you call that extraordinary,' said the White Cat. 'Or remarkable. Or fantastic. I don't.'

He walked slowly to the airing cupboard, and curled himself up in a clean blanket.

'You might put a notice on the door,' he murmured sleepily. 'DO NOT DISTURB. Thanks. Good night!'

DRAGONRISE
Kathryn Cave

What do dragons like to eat best? – GIRLS! When the dragon under Tom's bed told him this, Tom became worried that the poor thing must be starving. Then Tom's elder sister, Sarah, did something that Tom could not forgive – and he realized that the dragon could help him to take a very unusual revenge!

THE WORST WITCH
THE WORST WITCH STRIKES AGAIN
A BAD SPELL FOR THE WORST WITCH
Jill Murphy

Mildred Hubble is the most disastrous dunce of all at Miss Cackle's training school for witches. But even the worst witch scores the occasional triumph.

TWO VILLAGE DINOSAURS
Phyllis Arkle

Two dinosaurs spell double trouble as Dino and Sauro trample their amiable way through the village, causing chaos and confusion on every side.

BRIDGET AND WILLIAM
Jane Gardam

Two horses, two children and two stories of hill farm life. Bridget had William, a shaggy Shetland pony, as round as a partridge, and she was determined to keep him. Susan had Horse, an utterly huge white horse, two hundred years old, cut out of the hillside – and she was determined to save him.

OLGA TAKES CHARGE
Michael Bond

Disaster has struck and Olga da Polga happens to be the only one around who can take charge and save the world – or so she thinks.

TOTTIE: The Story of a Dolls' House
Rumer Godden

The Plantagenets don't believe they'll ever move out of their draughty shoe-box, but their owner are given an antique dolls' house like the one Tottie remembers. The dolls are delighted with their new home until haughty Marchpane, a selfish china doll, moves in with them and acts as though she owns the place.

THE ANITA HEWETT ANIMAL STORY BOOK

A big collection of cheerful, funny and fascinating stories about animals from every corner of the world. Discover how the Platypus family find a suitable home, why small Gorilla only want parsley for dinner, what happened to Rhino's hat, and how the Yellow Jungle Frogs find a use for their noisy singing and dancing.

THE DEAD LETTER BOX
Jan Mark

Louis got the idea from an old film which showed how spies left their letters in a secret place – a dead letter box. It was just the kind of thing that she and Glenda needed to help them keep in touch. And she knew the perfect place for it!

THE PERFECT HAMBURGER
Alexander McCall Smith

If only Joe could remember *exactly* what he had thrown so haphazardly into the mixing-bowl, he knew that his perfect hamburger could revive his friend Mr Borthwick's ailing business and drive every other fast-food store off the high street.

Who is he?

His name is Smudge, and he's the mascot of the Junior Puffin Club.

What is that?

It's a Club for children between 4 and 8 who are beginning to discover and enjoy books for themselves.

How does it work?

On joining, members are sent a Club badge and Membership Card, a sheet of stickers, and their first copy of the magazine, *The Egg*, which is sent to them four times a year. As well as stories, pictures, puzzles and things to make, there are competitions to enter and, of course, news about new Puffins.

For details of cost and an application form, send a stamped addressed envelope to:

The Junior Puffin Club
Penguin Books Limited
Bath Road
Harmondsworth
Middlesex UB7 0DA